SECOND

ONE

HUNDRED

Future Chron Universe

Volume 24

To The Stars Series

Book 3

D.W. PATTERSON

Eleventh Printing – May, 2023

1

5.14.2643

The audio alarms aboard the fusion ship *Iapyx* sounded. It was an old fashioned warning system but still quite effective when humans were involved. The only problem was that the humans aboard were unconscious. They had been rendered that way by a phenomenon of wormhole travel that had not been encountered before. It was like driving into a wall at sixty miles an hour but with physiological consequences instead of physical.

Dr. Jackson, a physicist and astronomer, was the first to wake from the trauma.

At first, Sheila Jackson thought she was in her apartment back, where?

Strange I remember my apartment but not where it is.

Except the room was too small to be her apartment and the bed was a single instead of a full and the lights were overhead instead of a lamp beside the bed and ...

Sheila sat up. Where was she? Her mind started racing. She felt almost panicky, she wanted to flee. But where?

Maybe her Emmie would tell her something, where was it? She looked around. There it was on the small table in the corner of the room.

She moved to the table and picked up the device which was like a personal assistant with an Em based AI. (Em standing for emulated brain. A human brain emulated in a computer). She unfolded the Emmie until its screen was large enough.

Sheila said, "Emmie where are we?"

The Emmie was slow to respond which was uncharacteristic.

"Unknown," is all it said.

Sheila's feeling of panic changed to curiosity, her defining characteristic.

How could my Emmie not know where we are?

"Emmie do a diagnostic level one please."

While she waited for the results Sheila looked about the room. There was a food processing center next to the table in the corner. The bed was across the room from there and the reading lamp was attached to the wall instead of on the nightstand like in her apartment. There was what looked like a small row of lockers built into the wall at the foot of the bed. They framed a door.

To where?

There was also a door on the remaining wall. Sheila assumed one door led to a bathroom. Where the other one led she didn't know and at the moment didn't want to know.

The Emmie finished the diagnostics and began announcing the results. Sheila interrupted it when it got to memory capacity.

"Emmie, excuse me for interrupting, but what is the start time of the current memory block aggregation?"

By aggregation, Sheila meant the continuous recording of events by the Emmie.

"Memory begins sequencing from oh-three-hundred."

"And the time now?"

"Oh-three twenty-two."

Sheila was a bit stunned.

The same memory of time I have but a completely different type of substrate.

Sheila meant that whatever had happened had affected both their memories, hardware and wetware, the same. She and the Emmie both suffered from memory loss. Whatever was wrong, it wasn't just Sheila, it was more widespread and affected equipment as well as humans.

But thinking about the Emmie's memory loss brought Sheila back to the question. Where was she?

She would have to see what was beyond the doors. She chose the door near the foot of her bed because she thought it most likely to be the bathroom. It was and though small it looked to be sufficient.

Leaving the bathroom she looked at the remaining door in the room. Wherever she was, she would have to go through that door to find out.

She approached the door. She noticed it was different from the bathroom door, it was without an obvious door handle but there was a sensor pad next to it on the wall. The only thing she could think of was to hold the palm of her hand up to the sensor.

Before her hand touched the pad it worked. The door recessed into the wall. It was obviously not a touch sensor but operated optically.

She went through and found herself in a long hall that curved peculiarly upward as one looked into the distance. The door closed behind her. She looked one way and then the other and then turned to walk down the hall.

There were other doors like hers, all on one side of the hall. They each had their pads. She tried a couple but the doors didn't open. As she continued the doors grew further and further apart, obviously the rooms behind them were getting larger but still none opened for her.

Then she came to an open door.

Open but why?

She saw a person's foot in the door but that was all. She hesitated. Forcing herself to look she saw the still form of the man belonging to the foot. Poking her head further into the room she saw other bodies either lying on the floor or collapsed in chairs, both men and women.

Their Emmies lay beside the bodies. Other equipment in the room seemed to be working as there were sounds and lights and images on the screens. As Sheila entered further into the room she was able to turn and see a great wallscreen. The view down a central girder to a large bulk was in stark relief to the dark background. Except it wasn't completely dark, there were lights in the blackness, pinpoints of lights as if viewed from the observatory back in the Centauri Two habitat.

Suddenly Sheila knew where she was from and where she was now. She was from the Centauri System on a fusion ship bound to . . . *Where?*

2

5.1.2643

It started as a bet. A bet that should have never been made.

Captain Jenkins was betting with his First Officer.

"Mac I'll bet you that we can make it in one jump. I've studied all the reports on this enhanced wormhole drive. They've never been used at full power and still they make forty light-years at a time."

"Captain, you aren't suggesting that we use full power to make this jump are you?"

"No. We won't need full power. I figure ninety-eight point two-five percent should do it."

"That's awful close to full power Captain. No one has ever used more than ninety percent. That's recommended, in the book."

"The book don't make you famous Mac."

5/13/2643

The *Iapyx,* which meant N*orth Wind*, was a fourth generation-plus fusion ship outfitted to carry one hundred settlers to the Trilos System, forty-seven light-years from Earth or forty-two point seven light-years from the Centauri System from which the *Iapyx* would launch.

Sheila Jackson would be aboard the *Iapyx*. Her dual doctorates in Astronomy and Physics would make her the go-to person if any of these disciplines were needed. Until then in the spirit of the expedition, she would be standing watch over the fusion engines. She knew a lot of theory about both the fusion engines and wormhole drive but didn't have a lot of practical experience. The drive techs tried to make that apparent as she trained.

"Now Dr. Jackson," said tech Harris. "What would happen if the cast of the far wormhole mouth were to fail?"

"The near wormhole mouth that had been enlarged out of the quantum foam would tend to collapse."

"That's correct Dr. Jackson as far as it goes but don't forget that any link that was being forged in the wormhole dimension would also tend to collapse upon itself."

"And the resultant pileup," continued Sheila, "of exotic matter at this end would cause the near wormhole mouth to increase in size."

"That's correct. And if we aren't careful the size of the wormhole mouth could enlarge enough to swallow the ship."

"And might cause," continued Sheila, "a dangerous bounce in the size of the mouth which would also damage the ship."

"Very good Dr. Jackson. Most theorists aren't well versed on the operational realities of the wormhole drive."

"Well I like to ground my theory in practical realities."

Harris shook his head approvingly.

There was a more serious problem with creating a wormhole mouth than a failed cast. The energy required to open and expand a microscopic wormhole out of the vacuum was so great that if misapplied it could cause a breakdown in spacetime. The particle entanglements that led to the emergence of space could be sundered by an intense beam of energy microscopically focused. Such a disruption of spacetime gave rise to an expanding sphere of destruction which fortunately dissipated over distance. The distance of ten astronomical units or ten AU was thought enough for such a disruption caused by a single ship to dissipate, so all ships had to boost to this quarantine limit before using the wormhole drive. It usually took fourteen days at maximum acceleration/deceleration for a fourth generation-plus ship.

It was a busy time for the fusion engineers. Standing continuous watch caused them to be physically exhausted. Dr. Jackson was one of those on the duty roster. Because of the illness of another engineer she had just come off a sixteen-hour watch.

"You must be exhausted Dr. Jackson," said Harris.

"I am."

"Well the good news is we are almost there, one more eight-hour shift and we should be at the quarantine limit. You should just get some rest."

"That's my plan," said Sheila. "I'll see you on the other side."

Sheila headed straight for her quarters. She would have a small meal there and go straight to bed. She was still asleep when they made the jump.

5/14/2643

Sheila's first thought after discovering the control room was to figure out the location of the ship. She walked across the room to the consoles. She looked for navigation, the NAV console. Finally figuring out the right console she rolled the limp body of the console's crew member to one side and asked her question of the NAV Em.

"NAV location please."

A long moment.

"Unable to comply with request."

It figures, why should anything be working?

"NAV can you tell me why you are unable to comply?"

"NAV database has no reference."

What in the world? It should be full of references.

"NAV run a diagnostics."

Another long moment.

"Complete."

"How many stars are in your star database?"

"None."

Okay, that's a problem. NAV Em is wiped just like me and my Emmie. I'll need to find the datacube backup.

Sheila thought but couldn't remember where the datacubes were kept.

How strange the things I remember and the things I forget.

She started to look for them but then realized that they would probably be stored behind a sensor padlock just like her door.

The Captain or First Officer would be needed to trigger the pad.

First, she would have to find the datacube locker, then she would have to find the Captain or First Officer and drag them close enough to the sensor pad to use their palm to open datacube storage.

She had been at it for over an hour looking for a central depository for the datacubes in the command room. She had been around the room several times when she suddenly felt very tired. Bone tired. She collapsed in a corner and began to cry. Asking for someone, anyone to help her. She carried on for several minutes, she prayed and then she stopped.

That makes sense. It would be better than putting them all in one place in case of an accident. Distributed, they would not all be destroyed if the repository was damaged.

She made her way back to the NAV console. Rolling the crew member over near the console she hesitantly grasped her hand

and dropped it immediately. The hand was warm, not cold as Sheila expected. She felt for a pulse but couldn't make one out. She wasn't a doctor but surely the body should be cold by now.

After staring at the still form for a minute she continued. When the crew member's palm approached the sensor pad suddenly the console came alive. Apparently from the readout, the datacube was already installed and all she needed to do was tell the NAV Em to restore.

After a few moments, she asked again where the ship was located in relation to the Centauri System. The Em again uncharacteristically hesitated. Finally, it spoke.

"Forty-seven point one light-year distant . . ."

The Em continued giving information but Sheila tuned out.

Forty-seven light years away from any help. We've jumped way beyond the usual limits and who knows what condition the wormhole drive is in?

Sheila felt completely defeated. She had to get back to her quarters if she could.

3

Over the next wake-sleep cycle Sheila got most of command restored. Having to move the inert bodies, which for some unknown reason maintained their warmth even though Sheila couldn't detect any sign of life, either breath or pulse, was a challenge for a person her size.

She had decided to move the bodies from the control room into the infirmary. Even though the artificial gravity of the rotating crew wheel was four-tenths that of Earth it was all she could do to drag the larger bodies. In the infirmary were only the doctor and nurse. Sheila was unable to lift some of the bodies onto the beds or gurneys so she left them on the floor and covered them with sheets. The sight of all those bodies laid out and covered with white was not one she wanted to remember.

Feeling as if she had done all she could for the victims of whatever had befallen the ship Sheila sat in the control room to plan her next steps.

Ideally, she would use the wormhole drive to head back to the Centauri system. She knew theoretically all the steps required to open a near wormhole mouth and to cast the far wormhole mouth but she had never operated the drive herself. She was more familiar with the fusion engines. So getting the wormhole drive to work would be a challenge.

As a backup plan, she could continue the mission to Trilos which would be closer than Centauri. In that system she had a choice between two Earth-like planets. The shuttle could put her down on one of them automatically but then what?

She would live the rest of her life alone on a strange planet. And how long would a life like that last?

Sheila closed her eyes and shook her head. Every time she tried to think through her situation she always ended up alone. For the rest of her life, alone. She had never thought about it before. But now that it was a possibility it seemed to be the endpoint of all her thoughts.

It had been a long day of hard work. Between the physical exertion and the seeming hopelessness of her situation, she found herself without the stamina to continue for the day. She retired early.

Sheila heard the noise through the closed door of her quarters. She sat up in bed and faced the door. Another bump was heard from the hall. She was sure now she wasn't dreaming.

Sheila jumped out of bed and ran to the door. Opening the door she walked out into the hall and looked. No one was there, she listened. She heard nothing and then far down the hall came another bump like someone was carrying something and had hit one of the walls.

Sheila moved as fast as she could in the direction of the sound.

First she saw the person's feet as the slight curve of the ceiling hid the rest of the body. She wasn't certain but it looked like a man's boots. And he was dragging something. As she got closer he stopped, apparently hearing her coming.

Sheila slowed. When she could finally see his head she said hello in a raised voice.

"Hello yourself," said the man. "Aren't you Dr. Jackson?"

"Yes that's right," said Sheila as she walked up to the man. "I'm sorry I remember your face but not your name."

"That's understandable," said the man. "I'm kind of in the background on this trip. I'm Olson MacGregor, chef and repairman."

"Yes, that must be it. I've seen you in the cafeteria. What is that you're carrying?"

"Oh, this is the meat processor. I thought I was all alone so I was moving it to the coffee shop, closer to my apartment for convenience."

"How long have you been awake?"

"I've been through a couple of sleep cycles I guess."

"Me too. I wonder how we missed each other?"

"I guess because I've mostly gone the opposite way around the wheel to get to the cafeteria."

"That would explain it."

"Speaking of explaining it, can you tell me Dr. Jackson, what's happened?"

"I don't know myself, Mr. MacGregor."

"Olson please."

"Of course, and I'm Sheila, not Dr. Jackson."

"Very well Sheila. I was just about to prepare a meal would you like to join me."

"Very much," said Sheila smiling.

Vat grown steaks, scalloped potatoes, a fresh salad from the aeroponic's garden and a glass of wine made up the meal. Sheila finished her plate and looked at the glass of wine.

"This is the first time since I woke up in this mess that I feel my anxiety subsiding."

"That's why I became a cook. There is nothing like a good meal to brighten your outlook."

"Speaking of this mess, what do you think we should do next Olson."

"You mean after a good night's sleep I assume."

"Yes," she said.

"Well we've got enough supplies and provisions to last two people for at least fifty years I figure. So we needn't panic. But I think we've got to figure out what happened to everyone. I don't think they are dead. Have you noticed how the bodies are still warm, maybe not as hot as normal but not cold?"

Sheila nodded.

"It looks like some form of hibernation to me. But how long they can stay that way I don't know. So if we can't figure out how to awaken them then we should try to get back and get some help. What do you think?"

"I think you are right. We need to do all we can for the rest of the crew even if that means going back."

She paused.

"Only problem is that while I know how the wormhole drive works theoretically, I don't have any practical experience with it. So I'm not sure I can get us back."

"Don't worry we'll cross that bridge when we come to it. Right now I want to secure the ship and see if I can awaken any of the sleepers aboard."

They talked for a bit longer, then Olson walked Sheila back to her quarters and said goodnight. They would meet the next morning in the coffee shop.

4

Sheila woke to the shaking. She looked at her Emmie it was almost oh-five-hundred. She turned her light on and sat up. She wasn't dreaming, the ship was undergoing a high-frequency vibration. She guessed a few hundred kilocycles per second.

She dressed and was making her way to control when she noticed a decrease in the artificial gravity and a diminishing of the vibrations. In control she found MacGregor at the life-support console. He looked up.

"Good morning Sheila. Did the shaking wake you up?"

"Yes, what is it? What's going on?"

"The crew wheel has developed a vibration. Probably the superconducting magnetic bearing. We are floating on a magnetic field, so something must have gone wrong in that circuit."

"I noticed a drop in artificial gravity."

"Yeah I slowed the spin-down until the vibration smoothed out. We have point-three Earth gravity now."

"I didn't expect you to know so much about the ship's systems."

"Well cooking was only part of my training. I was also trained as a technician on most of the ship's systems, except for the engines which you are the expert on," he smiled.

"Well I guess this expert will have some breakfast and get to work."

"Great let's eat."

After breakfast, they were in the control room at the wormhole drive controls.

"I think," said Sheila, "as a first test we should try to open a small communications wormhole and get a message back to Centauri about what has happened and what we are going to do. We can cast it all the way since such a small wormhole takes much less energy. If you'll prepare the communications I'll start the drive sequencing."

"Aye, aye, we'll get somewhere now," he said with a smile.

He moved to the communications console and using his Emmie on which he had a duplicate image of the comm officers palm he triggered the sensor and it authenticated and allowed entry. Olson just shook his head, as with most deterrents the sensors only kept out honest people. He began dictating a message.

Sheila had done the same at the drive console and started the wormhole drive. The first check was to see if the isotopic storage unit had enough power to open the wormhole. (Isotopic storage was a technology that used the atomic nucleus to store and release energy, it was thousands of times more compact and powerful than chemical storage.)

Though drained from the long jump there was still enough reserve to open a small wormhole mouth for messaging but for anything else they would have to find a way to recharge the isotopics. That meant orbiting the nearest star for its light and energy.

Sheila looked forward to starting and running the fusion engine about as much as she did the wormhole drive, which was not at all. Still, someone had to do it.

The wormhole drive consisted of three great rings of material grafted on to the outer hull of the spinning crew wheel. The drive used the Mach effect to concentrate a huge amount of negative mass-energy (sometimes called exotic) in a very small spot in space. The result was a repulsive gravitational force concentrated at a point in space.

At the quantum level, spacetime is a churning, frothing mix of all kinds of topological objects. Among these are tiny wormhole mouths created and destroyed according to the uncertainty relations for energy, higher energy, shorter existence. If a concentration of negative enfergy is focused on one of these microscopic mouths, the repulsive force could expand it to the macro level. The number of wormhole mouths blinking in and out of existence in the quantum foam was so great that the drive almost always found a candidate to expand on the first try.

Sheila was watching the wallscreen which showed the space in front of the ship. There she saw a bright point of light form. The point grew in size under magnification to about the size of a basketball. It then seemed to shimmer and crystallize into a sphere, clear but milky. Sheila cast the far wormhole mouth toward Centauri and sent the message before she noticed the increasing vibrations.

“Olson is that the wheel again?”

Olson had moved to the wheel control console when he felt the vibrations start.

“I don't think so. It seems to be a power surge.”

They were both so focused on the source of the vibration that they hadn't noticed the wallscreen. There the mouth had become opaque and was growing and coming closer and closer to the ship.

By the time Sheila noticed, it was too late, the globe that was the wormhole's mouth filled the screen and soon consumed the fusion ship and crew wheel. The effect was as if the artificial gravity had been neutralized. The exotic mass-energy that framed and supported the wormhole was affecting the crew wheel's gravity.

Sheila found herself weightless and beginning to drift as the small velocity difference between head and feet caused a rotation of her body. Luckily she was just beside the drive console's chair. She was scooped up by the chair, which being bolted to the deck, was traveling as fast as the spinning crew wheel, a tangential velocity of almost fifty miles per hour.

Olson was not as fortunate. He had spun almost horizontally before he could grab the corner of a console and work himself into its chair.

“Olson can you spin it down?”

“I think so.”

He used his Emmie to command the spin rate to slow down.

As it came to a stop Sheila spoke up.

"We're in the wormhole mouth and there doesn't seem to be any place to go. The far mouth must have collapsed."

"Did the message get out? What do we do?" said Olson. "Are we in any danger?"

"I don't know, no one has ever been in a mouth for very long. The physics of the wormhole dimension are still being figured out."

"Well let's not add to that quest. Let's get out of here."

"Okay. I'll have to start the fusion engines and nudge the ship forward a bit. We should then emerge from the mouth."

"Wouldn't it be easier to just turn off the drive and let the mouth collapse?"

"I don't know. But I remember that the physicist Emmy Gibbs used the wormhole mouth to compress matter in her experiments. So I'm not sure whether it would just dissipate or collapse to a singularity that would crush us in its infinite density."

Olson looked stunned.

"You mean we could be crushed to a point just because this wormhole mouth decided to increase in size and engulf the ship? That hardly seems fair."

"We're not dealing with a reasonable entity Olson. We're dealing with physics."

He wasn't mollified but said, "Okay, you just do what you think is best, you're the expert."

"Okay I'm going to try to start the fusion engines."

Olson wondered.

Why does she say try?

Sheila knew why she said try. Because no one had tried to run a fusion engine in a wormhole mouth before. Ships approaching a mouth always cut engines before entering the wormhole. No one knew what would happen to an operating fusion engine in the wormhole dimension.

Sheila moved slowly to the fusion drive console and brought it online. She entered the startup sequence into the drive's Emmie. She touched the screen to run the sequence.

Immediately the ship's frame groaned and popped as if under stress. Olson felt his insides ripple as if he were sick. His guts cramped. He yelled above all the noise.

"What's happening?"

"I don't know," said Sheila not loud enough for him to hear. She was feeling the same effects as Olson.

She reached to cancel the startup. Immediately the pain and nausea and noise stopped.

"What is it?" gasped Olson.

"I think we're stuck," said Sheila almost collapsing.

5

They had made their way with some difficulty from the control room to the coffee shop. Olson had trouble making something to drink in low gravity. Luckily he remembered that there were some squirt packs just for such a situation.

“I'm glad whoever provisioned this ship had more foresight than me,” he said. “I would never have thought to put aboard some rations for near zero-g operations.”

“Things haven't gone well have they?” said Sheila.

Olson looked at her with concern. Maybe she was reaching the end of her rope.

“Oh I don't know,” he said. “We're alive, we've got food and drink and power. Hey, why do we have power if we can't run the fusion engines?”

Sheila had her head in her hands but the question made her think instead of bemoaning the situation.

“That's a good question,” she said looking up at him.

“Right now with the engines down all our power is coming from the isotopics. That power though is quite a bit less than the power of the fusion engines. I suspect that the exotic energy holding the mouth open would also be sufficient for our current power needs if we need to recharge.”

“I see. And what caused our sickness?”

"The massive flux of power when the fusion engine starts destabilized the balance between normal mass-energy and exotic mass-energy and I think it must have generated intense but small ripples of spacetime as the mouth adjusted. The ripples passing through our bodies caused us to feel sick."

"So we can't use the fusion engines?"

"It looks that way."

"Great, this just keeps getting better and better. How are we going to get out of here then?"

They had returned to the control room and were going over the consoles for anything they might have missed.

Just then the wallscreen burst into light. The shaking and noise started again and Olson and Sheila felt sick.

"What is it?" cried Olson.

"I think the mouth just swallowed something."

"What?"

"I don't know. Probably a stray space rock."

The shaking started to diminish, they both began to feel better.

Olson wiped the sweat from his forehead.

"Are we going to have to go through that every time it swallows something."

"No, that was probably a very small mass. Anything larger and the effects will be much worse."

"Well I say we just turn off the wormhole drive and take our chances. It has to be better than our present situation."

"Well if the mouth does collapse instead of dissipate it will be a much faster death. We won't really know it as it will collapse at the speed of light."

"Good. Got my vote."

"Okay, here goes."

Sheila started to enter the shutdown sequence but then looked up rather sheepishly at Olson.

"What is it?" he said.

"The drive is already shut down. It shut down automatically when we reduced the spin of the crew wheel below the minimum needed. I should have realized it but at the time I wasn't thinking straight."

"If the drive is offline and has been for some time then what is keeping the wormhole mouth open?"

"My guess is that since the far mouth collapsed prematurely the exotic energy that would normally have been dissipated out the exit mouth is trapped in this mouth and is more than enough to keep it open. That is probably why it expanded and engulfed the ship."

"So now that we know what happened what do we do next?"

"The energy will eventually leak away due to quantum effects, just as a black hole evaporates due to Hawking radiation. Then the mouth should grow smaller and dissipate naturally and slowly. Leaving us in empty space."

"How long will that take?"

"Off the top of my head, without doing the calculations, I would say that it will take months for the wormhole to dissipate completely. But once it becomes small enough for the ship to start to emerge we should be able to use the fusion engines. That would cut the time by a month or more."

"Months? We can't wait here months. What happens to the rest of the crew while we vacation out here?"

"I don't know," Sheila said somewhat insulted. "I didn't say it was my preferred course of action. I was only answering your question."

"I know. I'm sorry if I seemed overly critical. But I'm tired of all these catch-22s. You know, we can't do this because of that, kind of thing."

"I understand. Why don't we take a break and rest? Maybe then I can think more clearly."

They agreed they had done enough for the day and would meet again the following day in the coffee shop.

Back in her quarters, Sheila had to first rearrange her bed for sleep in the near zero-gravity. She removed a rolled-up sleeping bag from storage unrolled it and began to anchor it to the corners of her bed. The bed and sleeping bag had been specially made for such an arrangement.

Once finished she went to the bathroom and reconfigured everything for there before she could finish her preparations for sleep. Climbing into the sleeping bag she noticed for the first time the strange sensation of near zero gravity. Although she had trained in it this was the first time she would have to sleep in it. It turned out to be difficult for her which was somewhat surprising as many others had sworn it was the best sleep they had ever had.

Sheila decided it was just the novelty of the situation and there wasn't anything physically wrong. She would just have to wait until her mind settled down and accepted the situation.

But that was the problem. She didn't accept the situation consciously or unconsciously. She was a problem solver and she had a problem to solve. So she lay there with the dim light of the room becoming brighter and brighter as her eyes adjusted.

There must be some way out of this mess. I should have paid more attention, we wouldn't be here in the first place if I had. I could have moved the ship easily before the mouth engulfed us. It wouldn't even have taken the fusion engines just a little attitude control...

She stopped and tried to sit up before she realized she had zipped herself pretty tightly into the bag. She unzipped the sleeping bag to her waist and then sat up.

The attitude rockets, I can use the attitude rockets to give us a small velocity without upsetting the energy equilibrium of the mouth unduly.

Sheila lay back but had a hard time going to sleep as her mind calculated the proper firing sequence and duration to accomplish her goal.

6

The next morning Sheila was thirty minutes late in meeting Olson at the coffee shop.

"There you are," he said.

Sheila walked carefully through the door and using the handholds in the wall pulled her way to the table where Olson was seated.

"You look tired. Didn't you sleep well?"

"I did after I fell asleep but it took some time to accomplish that."

"Couldn't get used to the low-g?"

"No, I was thinking. I think I've come up with a way to get us out of here."

"Really?"

"Yeah we have other propulsion systems aboard this ship besides the fusion engines."

"Other propulsion?"

"Yeah, you know. The attitude rockets."

"Of course, why didn't I think of that."

"Because we both have been somewhat overwhelmed by the situation, I expect. I know I have and it's affected my reasoning."

"Yeah, me too. Although even if I had thought about it I would have expected the same reaction to using them as the fusion engines."

"Oh there will be a reaction from the mouth but at the small velocity we need to break out I don't think it will be nearly as dramatic as starting the fusion engines. The time rate of change of energy is magnitudes less with the attitude rockets and therefore the reaction of the mouth should be magnitudes less."

"Great. I really didn't want to go through that sick feeling again."

Sheila shook her head in agreement.

After breakfast, they went to the control room. Sheila moved to the attitude rocket's console. She tried to use her Emmie to sign in but failed.

"What's wrong?" asked Olson.

"The sensor pad is not taking this hand print."

"You sure you are using the right one?"

"I'm using the one you marked as attitude rockets console."

"Oh."

"I wonder if you used the wrong hand?"

"I don't know. How was I supposed to know which hand he used to sign in?"

"Okay. Do you remember who was at this station?"

“I haven't a clue. I did so many hand prints that they all run together.”

“Okay I'll just run through all the ones we've recorded.”

None of the prints worked.

“Okay, his identity will be in the crew records. All we have to do is search them.”

But a query of the crew records returned a worrying result.

“Are you sure?” said Olson.

“Yes. The Emmie says those records do not exist. It's the same as our memories and our personal Emmies. They've been erased.”

“What do we do now?”

“I don't know Olson, I don't know.”

All Sheila knew was that she had to get away from Olson to think clearly.

“I'm going back to my room for a rest. I will see you at dinner.”

Sheila turned before he could respond and was out the door. Back in her room, she climbed into her sleeping bag. She began to tear up but stopped. She had to think and crying, however much it might soothe her fears, wasn't going to help her think.

If only Olson hadn't messed up the hand printing.

She stopped herself. Blaming Olson wasn't going to solve the problem. The problem was they needed to get those rockets operating and eject a little reaction mass to move the ship.

A little reaction mass, I wonder.

Sheila awoke in the dark. The only light she had was her Emmie's screen. Using it she was able to make her way to the door but there she was stopped. Neither voice commands nor the sensor to open the door would respond.

Sheila panicked for a moment, but then remembered that part of her training for the mission, instructed her on how to manually open a ship's door. Using the Emmie's light she opened the access panel in the wall next to the door and began hand cranking the door open.

Once in the hall, she hurried to meet Olson at the coffee shop. He was there standing outside.

"The door won't budge," he said. "And I can't get my coffee."

"I hope that's the worst of our problems," said Sheila. "I don't know how you planned to make coffee anyway, without power."

"Yeah I see what you mean. How are we going to get the power back on?"

"Well first I'm going to open this door and have a snack, a pastry that doesn't need heating. And then I'm going to isotopics to see if there is anything that can be done to get some power back online."

Sheila removed the access hatch and proceeded to open the door. Unlike crew's quarters, public rooms had emergency access on both sides of the door.

After eating they went to isotopics where everything looked okay but the reservoir was badly drained.

“What now?” said Olson. “Nothing we do seems to work.”

Sheila could sense that Olson was becoming unhinged by the situation. She had to keep her wits and not panic. No telling what he would do if she showed the anxiety she felt.

“Well I've got an idea. It came to me last night. I think I can get us enough velocity to get out of this wormhole mouth.”

“Really?” said Olson his voice becoming calmer.

“Yeah. It has to do with the shuttles.”

“But they're as dead as the isotopics. Aren't they? And neither one of us could pilot one of them. I doubt we could even board one of them.”

“Well we don't have to board them or pilot them. We stay on the ship but use them to give us the momentum we need to escape the mouth.”

“How?” said Olson, looking at Sheila as if she had gone crazy.

“I don't know if you remember, but in training we learned how to launch the shuttles even from a disabled ship.”

"Yeah you're right, I remember. But how does that help our situation?"

"The launch mechanism is mechanically loaded so that a shuttle can be launched without power. And when the force of the launch reacts against the ship it should give us just enough momentum to slip through the wormhole mouth's boundary."

"Action, reaction, I get it now. What are we waiting for? Let's do it."

7

The shuttle release mechanism was halfway down the central girder of the ship where the shuttles were attached. Unlike older fusion ships the central spine was enclosed but not pressurized. It would still require a spacewalk to get to the release point.

Olson had experience with spacewalks having taken several on previous flights. Though Sheila had trained in the spacesuit and was confident she could do the job, she was nervous.

"Don't worry this is a piece of cake," he said to Sheila. "We don't even have to worry about losing our grip and drifting off into space. We'll be back before you know it."

Olson operated the airlock manually.

The quarter-mile journey would take a few minutes. The six shuttles were arranged around the spine at sixty-degree intervals, each with its own manual release. There were enough shuttles to evacuate the ship if needed.

Sheila was explaining again the need to release the two shuttles as close to the same time as possible.

"Because if we are out of sync too much we will give a spin to the ship and not acquire the forward momentum we need."

"Yes I understand Newtonian physics Sheila."

"Okay I'm just saying."

They were quiet for some time while they pulled themselves along the belt line. Ordinarily, the belt line would be pulling them along, but without power they had to muscle their way down the ship's spine. Finally, they arrived at the shuttle station. Sheila took one side while Olson took the other.

"Okay dial the launcher to its maximum deflection possible," said Sheila. The launchers were capable of being dialed to a launch angle of anywhere from thirty degrees away from the front of the ship to thirty degrees off the rear. For this launch, Sheila wanted both shuttles launched to the rear offset.

Once finished manually dialing in the deflection angle Sheila called Olson.

"You ready?"

"Ready."

"Three, two, one, release!"

Sheila felt herself being kicked by the ship as her launcher reacted. Then almost immediately the ship lurched the opposite way. There was no more than a second between each kick. Sheila hoped that would be close enough.

With the spacewalk finished they were making their way back along the girder to the crew wheel. Sheila, feeling as if a load had been lifted from her shoulders, for the first time took a real look at the spacetime they were in. It was as if there was an indeterminate sky above her, luminous with a soft white light. As she stared at the "sky" she saw darker streaks race across it. She wondered if that was not the exotic energy girder-like net that kept the mouth open, adjusting itself to the ever-changing stresses caused by the always shifting mass-energy balance. All in all, it had a calming effect on her nerves.

Back inside the crew wheel, there was nothing they could do but wait. And without power, they couldn't determine course or speed if any. Sheila figured that it would take at least eight hours before they would know anything. She said goodnight to Olson and retired to her quarters.

Sheila was awakened by a pounding on the door. She looked at the time on her Emmie. She had only been asleep four hours. She dressed and opened the door.

"Stars Sheila, I see stars. Your idea worked!"

"It's too soon Olson, unless."

Sheila took off for the control room.

"What Sheila, what is it?"

"If we are really out of the wormhole mouth then the wormhole is shrinking faster than I expected. And if it is, that could be the end."

"The end of what?" asked Olson.

"Us," she replied.

She explained to Olson the problem as they made their way to control.

"You see Olson, if we are out of the wormhole mouth this soon I suspect the mouth is shrinking faster than I expected. And if that is true then we could be in trouble."

"In trouble, how could we be in trouble? We just got out of trouble, didn't we?"

"Yes, but we could be in worse trouble. You see a wormhole mouth when left to itself will evaporate in much the same manner as a black hole. And at the very end of its life, a wormhole mouth will finish evaporating with an intense output of particles and energy. Putting it simply, if we are in the vicinity of this mouth when it evaporates we will be engulfed in an explosion."

"You're right that's worse. So what can we do?"

"Well we will manually connect the isotopics to the charging arrays and start renewing their charge with the energy and light given off by the wormhole. As it gets smaller and smaller that energy will increase and the charging of the isotopics should also occur at an increasing rate. When we have enough power reserves we will make a short jump to put distance between us and the wormhole mouth."

"But you said you didn't know how to use the drive."

"I know but we haven't any choice."

"Won't the distance decrease the charging rate?"

"Yes but not as much as usual because the energy output of the wormhole mouth will be increasing in an exponential manner so the isotopics will keep charging even at a considerable distance."

As with everything aboard a fusion ship, provision had been made to provide a manual method of tying in the isotopics to the solar arrays. Once the task was accomplished Sheila and Olson retired to their quarters for a rest.

Sheila woke to find her night light shining in her eyes. She must have left it on by mistake. As she reached to turn it off she stopped.

The light's on.

Sheila jumped out of bed and headed for control. Olson was already in the room. The consoles were powered, Olson was at work rebooting them. Sheila pulled her way to the power monitor.

"I've got the attitude console booted Sheila I found the correct print."

"Great Olson. We should have just enough power to run the electrics. But that means we can now aim the chemicals in the direction we want to go. It should put a little distance between us and the mouth. And I won't have to use the wormhole drive in an emergency situation."

She moved to the attitude control rockets, oriented them and set them for a ten-minute burn.

"Just ten minutes?" said Olson.

"Yeah we don't want to burn through all our fuel without being able to replace it. We'll still need attitude control when the fusion rockets come online."

"When will that be?"

"When the power levels reach twenty-five percent."

"We're at ten now."

"Yeah."

"What do we do until then?" asked Olson.

"Well I'm going to get something to eat and wait," said Sheila as she turned for the door.

In the nearby coffee shop, Sheila and Olson were still eating when they felt the shaking.

"What's that?" said Olson.

Just then an alarm went off. Sheila checked her Emmie.

"It's a radiation warning. Let's get to control."

As she entered the control room Sheila took a look at the wallscreen.

"That's not right," she said aloud.

The wallscreen was still focused on the wormhole mouth. Instead of a milky white light, the mouth was a patchwork of darker splotches moving beneath the surface. Sheila was sure that it was smaller than when they had first left for the break room.

“Can you get me a reading on the radiation environment?” asked Sheila.

“A huge spike, we just got our yearly quota. It's rising again.”

“Yes and we've got damage too. Some of the aft electronics are fried.”

“How?”

“Plasma wave hit us. The mouth is acting like a flare star but with a greater particle capacity. It's building a huge magnetic field and when it collapses it sheds the mass-energy as a plasma of particles.”

“I've never heard of such a thing.”

“Neither have I but I do know we can't survive too many more of those flares.”

8

"**M**aybe we should just take one of the shuttles and take our chances. We can leave the ship on automatic and recover it later when it has put enough distance between itself and the wormhole mouth," said Olson.

"If we could pilot a shuttle and if the ship reaches a safe distance before that mouth explodes."

"Well then more reason to get out."

"I can't leave the others," said Sheila.

"We don't even know if they will ever recover, maybe they are already dead."

"We recovered and I expect they will also if we keep the ship in one piece. It's like hibernation, they aren't dying."

"But we can't take those particle flares much longer. What can we do?"

"We can hope that we put enough distance between ourselves and that mouth before it explodes."

Less than two hours later there was another radiation alarm. Watching the wallscreen Sheila could see the wormhole mouth shrink and then rebound in size.

Collapse, that's how it generates the energy necessary for these particle storms.

She looked at the power readings, they were at fifteen percent.

Not enough to make a jump. Not enough to make much of a run on the fusion engines but we've got to do something.

Then the wormhole mouth brightened considerably.

"Olson turn the ship one-hundred eighty degrees!"

Olson started to ask why but after several days with Sheila he knew she was always right. So he didn't hesitate to move to the attitude rocket console and have his Emmie program the burn.

Sheila was already at the console controlling the front magnetic generator. The generator created a magnetic "bubble" in front of the ship to guide any charged particles around the *Iapyx* when it was in flight. The generator along with the front mass-plate stopped almost all particle incursions when at speed.

As the ship came around the particle storm hit. The wallscreen lit up in an aurora of colors as the charged particles slammed into the magnetic field lines giving up some of their energy as visible light. Repeatedly, over and over as in waves the lights danced in front of the ship until finally, they diminished.

"Hear that Olson?"

"What Sheila?"

"No radiation alarms."

"What's the power levels?"

"Twelve percent and building."

"So we made it," said Olson grinning.

"Not yet but our chances just improved."

Hours later the wormhole mouth, invisible without magnification on the wallscreen, started its last flare. As it collapsed and evaporated it released all its mass as an energy stream of light and particles. Momentarily brightening to a brilliant star-like intensity it was just as quickly gone. The particle shower hit the *Iapyx* seconds later. If not for the distance and the magnetic and physical barriers the rain of particles would have destroyed all life aboard and much of the electronics. As it was the ship and crew came through with only a few percent loss in power levels which was well over twenty-five percent now.

Sitting in the coffee shop Sheila was explaining to Olson why they should now make for Trilos.

"It's the closest star system to our location. I propose to make a short jump there. Once in system, we'll use our remaining power to put us into orbit."

"You are sure we can decelerate into the system?"

"I think so. I think I can at least get us close enough to the star to recharge even if not in a perfect orbit."

"Don't worry," came a voice from the doorway, "I can get us into a perfect orbit."

They both pivoted to see First Officer Mac Jones standing there.

“But I'd like to have something to eat first,” he said.

Olson fixed the First Officer some food while he and Sheila filled him in on their situation.

“So I've been asleep for almost two weeks? No wonder I'm so hungry,” he said as he finished another plate Olson had made.

“Fine food Mr. MacGregor,” he said sincerely. “Okay let's get started. I'll handle the navigation Sheila if you'll do the jump.”

Sheila shook her head and responded in the affirmative.

They all went to control and before long had the ship in the Trilos system.

“If you all want to get some rest I'll stand the first watch while the ship slips into orbit. I don't think I'll be needing any sleep for a while.”

Sheila and Olson agreed and retired to their quarters. Sheila was feeling more optimistic than she had felt in weeks and slept soundly.

When she woke she dressed and headed to control.

“Ah Sheila,” said Jones. “You remember Dr. Griffin?”

“Of course, hello doctor how are you?”

“I seem to be fine Dr. Jackson although my muscles are a little stiff.”

“Dr. Griffin do you know what happened to us?” asked Sheila.

"Not really Dr. Jackson. I can only guess. I was reviewing the early records of the trip when you came in. It appears that we went through a slight phase change because of the distance that we jumped and it affected our physiology.

"In essence our brains, under the strain of the physical change, essentially shutdown. The phase change space did not quite become the impenetrable barrier that was encountered early in the use of the wormhole drive. Instead the effect of the phase change in us was almost completely confined to a variation in the permeability of the blood-brain barrier. Larger molecules than normal were able to cross into the brain where they proved toxic to one degree or another.

"I suspect that the toxicity somehow affected our nervous systems putting us into a kind of hibernation. Very interesting effect if we can figure it out."

"It was the Captain," said the First Officer. "He wanted to establish a wormhole jump record."

"It was deliberate?" said Sheila.

First Officer Jones only nodded.

By the time they settled into orbit around the star more than two dozen other crew members were awake. Dr. Griffin thought that all of them would awaken eventually. He had begun a system of intravenous feeding for the remainder so that they wouldn't suffer the worse effects of their long hibernation.

The First Officer put them in a perfect orbit to recharge the isotopics. It took less than three weeks at which time nearly all of the crew had awakened and the ship was back to normal. Except for the Captain. First Officer Jones had confined him to quarters. They were meeting to decide what if any action to take.

"I know that Captain Price made a poor decision," said the First Officer. "But I think we should wait until we get him back to Centauri and let them decide what punishment he should be assigned."

"Well I as much as anyone object to the Captain's actions," said Sheila. "But I will agree to your proposal First Officer."

Most of the others agreed also. The Captain would remain in confinement until the ship returned to Centauri where he would face any punishment deemed appropriate.

EPILOGUE

"That's impossible," said the First Officer. "No ship can jump that far."

The Nav Officer had spent the time while the isotopics recharged to get a manual fix on their position. His results did not agree with the Ems. Instead of being forty-something light-years from Centauri, he had calculated over five-hundred light-years.

"We need someone to double-check your calculations."

"I can't be off that much," said the navigator. "But if you want someone to check my work I suggest Dr. Jackson, she has the background."

The First Officer explained to Sheila what he wanted her to do.

She was able to quickly check the navigator's figures. And then she checked them again.

"No doubt about it First Officer. It's just as the navigator says."

"Well I still say it's impossible. But you two are the experts. We are orbiting a star almost five-hundred years from where we're supposed to be. I guess there's no reason to prepare for a return to Centauri. We can't provision for such a long journey. Simply couldn't pack enough into the ship even if we could keep the ship going that far and that long. I guess we will stay right here.

"But it is troubling that the Ems were in error. We will need to do a complete test of our systems and recalibrate if needed. If an Em can't be adjusted we will be forced to take it offline."

Later the First Officer went to release the Captain from confinement.

"Why you letting me out now Mac? We're no where near Centauri are we?"

"No sir we're not and we aren't going to be."

"What do you mean?"

After explaining the situation the First Officer continued.

"So you see there's no use for a First Officer or Captain. We're all settlers now."

They made their way to the second planet from the star which they had started calling New Trilos. Luckily it was habitable. The settlers were shuttled down to the surface. The *Iapyx* crew stayed aboard the ship. They weren't quite ready to face their exile and hoped to figure out a way to get back to Centauri eventually.

But for now, the original settlers prepared themselves and their provisions on the planet where they planned to live for the rest of their lives. The *Iapyx* may have landed them on the wrong planet but they would still set up a settlement. A settlement that carried the hopes and dreams of humanity to the stars.

AFTERWORD

The development of the wormhole drive is covered in more detail in my novel "Mach's Metric". Its use and extension are the subjects of the novels "Mach's Mission" and "Mach's Legacy."

For further insight into why the expedition was so far away from its target system see the novella "The Path."

More discussion about Ems and their culture can be found in the novella "To Tend And Watch Over."

ABOUT THE AUTHOR

D.W. Patterson lives in the USA with his beautiful wife Sarah. He studied physics and read classic science fiction in college and then worked for many years as an electronic design engineer.

Now he's trying to write stories like the ones he once loved. See his website dwpatterson.com for more information.

Hard Science Fiction – Old School.

Also By This Author:

The Future Chron Universe:

To date the Future Chron Universe has:

51 Amazon Top 100's

(15 in the Top 10)

In chronological order.

Volume numbers indicate Universe order.

Book numbers indicate Series order.

From The Earth Series

(Novellas except where noted):

Volume 1, Book 1 – *Whatsoever You Do*

Volume 2, Book 2 – *War Through The Pines*

Volume 3, Book 3 – *Vigilance*

Volume 4, Book 4 – *To Tend And Watch Over*

Volume 5, Book 5 – *Union*

Volume 6, Book 6 – *Circle Of Retribution*

Volume 7, Book 7 – *Freedom From Want*

Volume 8, Book 8 – *Break Up*

Volume 9, Book 9 – *Kuiper Station*

Volume 10, Book 10 – *The Cloud*

Volume 11, Book 11 – *First Interstellar* – A Short Novel

Wormhole Series

(Novels):

Volume 12, Book 1 – *Mach's Metric*

Volume 13, Book 2 – *Mach's Mission*

Open Space Series

(Short Stories):

Volume 14, Book 1 – *Open Space*

Volume 15, Book 2 – *The Old World*

Volume 16, Book 3 – *Insurrect*

Volume 17, Book 4 – *Second Beam*

Volume 18, Book 5 – *All For One*

Volume 19, Book 6 – *One For All*

Volume 20, Book 7 – *Shotgun*

Volume 21, Book 8 – *Allison*

To The Stars Series

(Novellas):

Volume 22, Book 1 – *First One Hundred*

Volume 23, Book 2 – *First Dark Ages*

Volume 24, Book 3 – *Second One Hundred*

Volume 25, Book 4 – *Second Dark Ages*

Volume 26, Book 5 – *Path Of The Long March*

Wormhole Series

(Novel):

Volume 27, Book 3 – *Mach's Legacy*

Robot Series

(Novels):

Volume 28, Book 1 – *Spin-Two*

Volume 29, Book 2 – *Robot Planet*

Volume 30, Book 3 – *The Lattice Of Space*

Time Series

(Novels):

Volume 31, Book 1 – *Time Wars*

Volume 32, Book 2 – *Time's End*

Volume 33, Book 3 – *Frozen Time*

The Remembered Earth Universe:

To date the Remembered Earth Universe has:

8 Amazon Top 100's

Cislunar Series

(Short Stories):

Volume 1, Book 1 – *US Tugs*

Volume 2, Book 2 – *Prototype*

Volume 3, Book 3 – *L1 Or Bust*

Volume 4, Book 4 – *Guidance Box*

Volume 5, Book 5 – *Air Brakes*

Volume 6, Book 6 – *View Point*

Volume 7, Book 7 – *Space Truck*

Volume 8, Book 8 – *Dark Side* – *In Progress*

The Manifold Earth Universe:

Volume 1, Book 1 – *The Realm* – *In Progress*

Don't miss out!

Visit the website below and you can sign up to receive emails whenever D.W. Patterson publishes a new book. There's no charge and no obligation.

https://books2read.com/r/B-A-DPWE-DIJJC

BOOKS 2 READ

Connecting independent readers to independent writers.

www.ingramcontent.com/pod-product-compliance
Lightning Source LLC
La Vergne TN
LVHW010504160826
845677LV00012B/2645